I0456939

DEATH'S EMBRACE

A Hunted Past, Second Chance, Supernaturally guided, Short Romance

TAROT FANTASIES
BOOK V

JAX WILDER

Death's Embrace

Tarot Fantasies Series
Jax Wilder

RAINBOW QUARTZ PUBLISHING

PUBLISHED BY RAINBOW QUARTZ PUBLISHING, EDMONDS WA, 98026

ISBN: 978-1-961714-43-4 FIRST EDITION: 2024

COVER DESIGN BY MIRANDA TOWNSEND

INTERIOR DESIGN BY MIRANDA TOWNSEND

TAROT CARD DESCRIPTION BY LORELAI HAMILTON FROM THE BOOK TEENAGE TAROT – USED WITH PERMISSION.

LIBRARY OF CONGRESS CATALOGING-IN-PUBLICATION DATA HAS BEEN APPLIED FOR.

FOR PERMISSIONS OR INQUIRIES, PLEASE CONTACT: RAINBOW QUARTZ PUBLISHING

RAINBOWQUARTZPUBLISHING@GMAIL.COM WWW.RQPUBLISHING.COM

For every person who's struggling with the loss of a loved one.

Jax Wilder

13. Death

"The caterpillar doesn't know the beautiful butterfly it will become. It is not the end, it's simply change" Death.

KEY WORDS AND PHRASES:
TRANSFORMATION AND REBIRTH

Endings and new beginnings
Letting go of the old to make way for the new
Release and surrender
Transition and change
Growth through adversity
Inner and outer renewal
Symbol of profound change
Embracing the unknown
The inevitability of change and impermanence

There's a dark figure on a horse, riding through a field of flowers. It might seem a little intense, but think of it as powerful. The Death card is all about shedding the old to make way for the new.

Sometimes things have to end in order for something new to begin. Death is about change and growth. Think of it like an end to one chapter of your life and the beginning of something even better.

—Lorelai Hamilton, author of *Teenage Tarot* and *Tarot Tales & Magic Spells*

DEATH.

Chapter One

S oft, pliant dough moved under my hands as I kneaded the sourdough. I stood at a counter in the kitchen of *Knead The Dough* bakery. The air was warm and inviting, just right for bread to rise, carrying the comforting aroma of yeast and flour. Amidst the constant waves of emotions I experienced each day, my ritual became a reliable anchor, keeping me grounded.

The creaking floors foiled Shae's sneaky attempts, betraying his every step. Quietly, he slipped into the room and enveloped me in a warm embrace from behind, his brawny arms providing a sense of security. I could feel the warmth of his body. Our hands effortlessly merged in the dough, fingers interlocking, perfectly synchronized in our shared task. His breath was on my neck, his voice a whisper in my ear. "I can't wait to marry you, Baylin."

Dorothea's descent down the stairs brought with it the jarring reminder of the harshness of reality.

Shae was dead.

I closed my eyes, fighting back the tears welling in my eyes and the tightness in my chest. It was always there. His absence was a constant ache in my chest, a reminder of the void he left behind. I've been struggling with the grief and the inability to move on from his death.

Everywhere I looked, I saw him.

I could feel him here with me.

Every moment of every day, a shadow loomed over me, reminding me that his death was my fault.

Part of me died with him, leaving a hollowness in my chest. I was lost and worse than that, Shae left me behind.

"Good Morning, Baylin!" Dorothea's sing song voice rang out into the bakery.

"Coffee's ready," I called out. "I tried a new recipe today. Let me know if it sells okay."

"Oh? What is it?" she asked, entering the kitchen, cup of coffee in hand.

"It's a lemon croissant. I prepared the lemon filling, which is a mixture of fresh lemon zest, sugar, and a touch of lemon juice, creating a bright, tangy paste that pairs perfectly with the rich dough. Then I spread a small amount of the lemon filling on each triangle, careful not to overdo it. Too much filling, and the croissant will lose its structure; too little, and it won't have that burst of lemony goodness."

"Stars above, that sounds good," she said.

I watched through the oven window as the croissants puff up, their layers separating and crisping to perfection.

When they finally come out of the oven, they're a sight to behold—golden brown, flaky, and just slightly caramelized around the edges. I let them cool for a few moments before drizzling a light lemon glaze over the top, adding an extra touch of sweetness and tartness.

"Do you want to take the first bite?" I offered. "It's always the best part. The outside is crisp and flakey, while the inside is soft and buttery, with a bright burst of lemon that cuts through the richness," I said.

Dorothea nodded vigorously, taking one onto a napkin. She took a bite and her eyes close in pleasure. "It's a little piece of heaven, isn't it?"

I smiled. "I'm glad you like it."

"Have you been over to The Arcane Room lately?" Dorothea asked.

"I've been before, but not the last six months. Not since..." I trailed off, unable to say the words out loud. Not since Shae's death.

"Why don't you head over there today? I have a feeling that Ms. Vesper has something extra special for you."

I raised an eyebrow. "Is that your way of saying you remembered my birthday?"

"That's my way of saying happy birthday," she said.

Shea and I used to frequent The Arcane Room. It's this little mystical shop that seemed to offer magic in a bottle at times, but in recent months, it was only a quick fleeting sense of peace. On days like today, when all I wanted was any semblance of peace, I was willing to take what I could get—from anywhere.

There was something mysterious about Ms. Vesper, the shop's owner, that made me suspect she was more than just an ordinary person. Like not the kind of new age witchy person most of her customers were. However, her presence was reminiscent of a genuine witch, emitting an unsettling and formidable force.

She made me nervous. Ms. Vesper always had a way of seeing through any façade. Her wisdom and kindness shined through the rainiest of days. Despite how nervous she could make people—she's definitely not the kind of woman I'd ever cross—Ms. Vesper managed to act as a healing balm to the wounded souls of this town. It seemed I was the first customer this morning.

"Good morning, Baylin," she said, greeting me with a warm smile and a soft voice. Her piercing gaze saw through the mask I was wearing. "What can I help you find today?"

"I shrugged. I'm just kind of looking," I said. "My boss suggested coming down because today is my birthday."

"Is that why your heart is heavy with the weight of the world? Is it an unhappy birthday?"

I didn't bother suppressing the laugh that bubbled up. "I'd love to not feel the weight of anything for a while. I'd like to go back to how it was before."

Ms. Vesper tilted her head to the side, a thoughtful expression crossing her face. She seemed to make a decision. She walked behind the counter and found a tarot deck. "Come here, child."

I obeyed.

After shuffling the cards, she spread them out on the desk, their vibrant designs catching the light. "Choose one."

"One?"

"Only one."

Running my fingers along the cards, I stopped at one randomly. The deck seemed to whisper my name, but my neglected tarot skills made me hesitate. Like everything else I loved, tarot seemed to fall to the wayside until I felt better. Only "better" never seemed to come. I pulled the card. "May I see it?" I asked before looking at it.

Ms. Vesper nodded.

My heart pounded and my hand trembled slightly as I flipped one over to reveal the Death card. My stomach knotted at the sight of it, just another reminder I didn't need. I handed it to Ms. Vesper.

Her eyes softened as she looked at the card. "The Death card signifies endings, transformation, and rebirth. It's not about physical death, but I don't have to tell you that. You read tarot."

I nodded, "It's okay, it's good to hear it from someone else."

"Death signifies is the end of a chapter and the start of something new. Unaware of its transformation, the caterpillar remains confined within its cocoon, oblivious to the butterfly it will soon become. When everything feels like it's coming to an end, it's important to remember that there's still more left to discover. When the caterpillar finally breaks free from its cage and takes flight, it experiences a newfound sense of freedom, ready to discover the world from new heights.

With a sigh of relief, I released the breath that I had been holding. Despite knowing she was right, the truth was hard to swallow and left a bitter taste in my mouth.

"I have something special I think you'd like," she said with a grin. "Would you like to try it? It could help ease your pain and offer you some much deserved peace."

"I guess? What do I have to lose?"

Ms. Vesper guided me to a small white room at the back of the shop. In the center was a leather, black chaise lounge. "Please, make yourself comfortable."

Removing my purse and my shoes, I got comfy on the couch.

She served me a cup of fragrant tea. "Drink this down. It will help you relax into the experience."

As I sipped the tea, Ms. Vesper closed her eyes, and she took a deep breath. Her voice was a relaxing melody as she chanted. "By the card of Death, I call for change, to end the old and free the range. With this brew and mystic art, heal the wounds and mend the heart. Through the veil, let her now pass, to find the love lost in the past. By this card, the path is shown, rebirth awaits. She is not alone."

As the final words left her lips, a gentle breeze seemed to stir in the small white room, and the surrounding air shimmered with a soft, iridescent glow. The feeling of being pulled into a dreamlike state was overwhelming, and a sudden wave of drowsiness washed over me, making it difficult to keep my eyes open.

When I found the strength to open my eyes again, I was no longer in The Arcane Room. I was back at the bakery. Only there were rainbow clouds instead of a roof.

As I ran my fingers along the counter, I could feel the slight roughness of the wood grain beneath my touch. It was solid, cold, and felt like home. The sound of the oven timer dinging prompted me to quickly and instinctively grab the contents. It was a tray of lemon croissants. I set them out on the cooling rack and moved to the dough, waiting to be turned into bread.

As someone moved closer to me, the floorboard let out a loud creak. I couldn't bring myself to look. Strong arms wrapped around my waist. Only today, when I reached for the hands holding me tightly, they were solid. Unlike in my dreams, they didn't vanish into thin air the moment I touched them.

Was it real?

I turned. My breath caught in my throat.

It was Shae.

He was the same in every way, just as I remembered him. His eyes were a warm blue and full of love.

He took my hand in his, the touch so familiar and so very real. He was solid under my touch. "Shae," I whispered, tears falling to my cheeks. "Is it really you?"

My heart skipped a beat when he smiled. "Yes, Baylin. It's really me."

Chapter Two

The warmth of Shae's arms enveloped me, grounding me—mind, body, and soul. I hadn't felt this much relief or joy since he died. My breath hitched, and my hands trembled as I reached to touch his face. Despite the evidence, I couldn't shake the feeling that this was simply a cruel trick of my grief-stricken mind. But he was solid, warm, and seemed to be real in this place.

"Shae," I whispered, tears cascading down my cheeks. "Is it really you?"

His eyes, those familiar, liquid blue eyes, met mine with a softness I had almost forgotten. "Yes baby, it's really me."

The tears came faster now, and I buried my face in his chest, letting the scent of him—woodsy with a hint of lemon—wash over me. He held me tighter, his hands rubbing soothing circles on my back.

"I've missed you so much," I managed to say

through my tear-filled sobs, my body trembling uncontrollably.

"I've missed you too, Bay," he replied, his voice a gentle caress. "But I'm here, now. Is this how you want to spend our time together?"

I pulled back slightly, needing to see his face, to memorize every line and curve all over again. "How? How is this possible?"

A wistful smile played on Shae's lips, a poignant mixture of happiness and sorrow. "This place, it's special. It's where souls come when they have unfinished business. When they're not ready to let go of their human life."

Unfinished business.

The words hung in the air between us, heavy with unspoken meaning. I nodded, still struggling to comprehend. "And what about us? What's our unfinished business?"

He took my hand, guiding me to one of the bakery's tables. We sat down, the wooden surface cool beneath my fingers. "Baylin, I've been waiting here for you, waiting to help you find closure. I can't move on until you do."

I swallowed hard, the reality of his words sinking in. I repeated the word "closure," its foreignness lingering on my tongue. "There are so many things I don't even know where to begin."

Shae squeezed my hand, his touch grounding. "Let's start by remembering. Remembering the good times, the love we shared."

A small, hesitant smile crept across my lips. "Remember when I got the job at the bakery, when it first opened? How we stayed up all night, covered in flour and laughing until our sides hurt?"

He chuckled, the sound like music to my ears. "I remember. And how you insisted on perfecting that cake recipe until it was just right."

"Which took forever. But I wanted to surprise Dorothea with an opening day cake," I added, a genuine laugh escaping my lips. "It was totally worth it."

"Best red velvet cake of my whole life."

"I seem to recall you also saying I'd made the worst red velvet cake of your whole life."

We both laughed at that, the warm memories wrapping tendrils around us, pulling us into a cocoon of love. We reminisced about the early days, our laughter, and our love, slowly piecing together the fragments of our shared past. The longer we spent talking, the more the bakery seemed to come alive around us, the dreamlike quality intensifying. It was as if our memories were infusing the space with warmth and light.

But there were dark memories too, ones I had tried to bury deep within me, tucked away in a box that I never wanted to open again. The day of Shae's accident loomed large, an unspoken shadow over our happiness. I hesitated, the words caught in my throat.

"Bay, you don't have to be afraid," Shae said gently, sensing my turmoil. "We need to face it together."

I took a deep breath, summoning the courage to confront the pain. "The accident," I began, my voice trembling. "It was my fault. If I'd only done something different. If I had been there to stop it. I could have stopped it."

Shae's expression softened, and he cupped my face in his hands. "It wasn't your fault. It was an accident, and nothing you could have done would have changed that."

"You don't know that. I could have done something. I should have been able to do something," a sob caught in my throat.

"None of it was your fault. Life is finite and my time was up. That is not on you."

"It doesn't change the guilt I feel," I whispered, tears falling to my cheeks again. "The pain of losing you was debilitating. It's been unbearable."

Shae leaned in, pressing his forehead to mine. "I know, love. I know. But holding onto that guilt isn't helping you. You're trapped, baby. Being stuck in the past is preventing you from moving forward. You pressed pause on your whole life and you being left behind."

His words struck a chord deep within me. It was then that realized this encounter, this miraculous reunion brought about by some witchy magic, was part of my healing process.

It was the Death card.

I've been reading tarot long enough to understand the implications of that card. I had to face my grief head-on, to let go of the guilt that had been suffocating me. It seemed impossible for me to do that.

"How do I let it go?" I asked, my voice barely above a whisper. Too afraid of the answer to find his eyes. "How do I let you go?"

"By accepting that it's time to move on, to find happiness again," Shea said softly, kissing my temple. "I want you to live your life, Baylin. I want you to realize all of your dream and find hippieness. You deserve to love again. I want you to have everything this world has to offer you."

I nodded, the weight of his words settling in my heart. "I want that too, Shae. I want to honor our love, I'm just not sure how. You're there in every breath I take. In every move I make."

"That's a song, baby."

A sob escaped me, "I knoooow," I cried. "It just felt really pertinent to the moment."

He smiled, his eyes filled with pride and love. "Then let's do it together. Let's find that closure and give ourselves the peace we both deserve."

At that moment, I knew this journey was just beginning. With Shae by my side, I felt a glimmer of hope. We'd faced everything together. We would face the pain, embrace the love, and find a way to move forward on our own paths.

We stood, hand in hand. Standing in this dream-like bakery, this realm where anything was possible, I realized it was our sanctuary. And within its walls, I would find the strength to heal, to let go, and embrace the future.

"Ready?" Shae asked, his smile the most beautiful thing I'd seen in six months.

"Ready," I replied, squeezing his hand. A whisper of rebirth filled the air, carried by the first flicker of peace. "Let's do this."

Chapter Three

We stepped out of the bakery, hand in hand, into a version of Coral Cove that shimmered with an ethereal glow. The streets of our town were familiar, the same town I walked every day for years, the same town I grew up in. And yet, it was strange, void of other life, and bathed in a twilight that seemed to stretch endlessly, casting everything with a soft, dreamlike hue. It was as if we were walking through a memory of what was —a place where time stood still.

"What's our first destination?" Shae asked, his voice filled with curiosity.

We strolled down the street, and I looked around, taking in the sights of our town, transformed by magic. We neared the park where we had our first date. Shae packed us a picnic and surprised me with a red rose in the basket. It's the place where I first fell for him.

In the distance was the Spellbound Stories bookstore. We spent our day off work lazily walking the aisles, and eventually choosing books for each other. We'd stop by Golden Chopstick and grab takeout, the taste of flavorful noodles lingering on our tongues. Then, we'd spend the whole rest of the day reading in each other's arms, the softness of the book covers beneath our fingertips.

At the end of Main Street was Joe's coffee shop. I used to spend nearly every morning after work, at Joes. Shae would meet me there, and spend time together before his later shifts. I haven't been back since... All the normal things felt wrong after Shae died. The looks of pity on everyone's faces were impossible to ignore.

We fell in love right here in this town. Every corner held a piece of our history, a fragment of the love we shared. And I'd been avoiding all of it for months. Even my radio show fell apart when I couldn't go on air without weeping into the mic. I let his death take everything from me.

"Let's go to the park," I said, my voice steady with determination. "I want to remember some of the good times."

Shae squeezed my hand before leading me toward Pope Marine Park. The scent of blooming flowers filled the air, their vibrant colors standing out against the magical twilight sky. As we walked, memories flooded me. We came to this place countless times over the years. Each step brought us closer to the past. A past we both cherished above all else.

We reached our favorite spot, a secluded area by the harbor, where the water was calm enough to reflect the sky in a mirrorlike way. Shae spread out a blanket, and we sat down. The world around us was hushed and tranquil, as if holding its breath. Waiting for whatever happens next.

I held my breath, too.

"Do you remember the first time we came here?" Shae asked, his eyes twinkling with amusement.

I nodded, a smile tugging at my lips. "You brought a basket full of my favorite snacks, a bottle of wine, and a single red rose. You wooed me by being your charming self. We ended up talking for hours until the sky turned a deep shade of indigo and the first stars began to twinkle."

"And then I surprised you with that silly little song I wrote on the spot," he added, chuckling. "I was so nervous, but you laughed and said it was the sweetest thing anyone had ever done for you."

"It was," I whispered, the memory warming my heart. "You always knew how to make me feel special."

We sat in silence for a long while, just playing with each other skin. Running fingers up and down, arms and backs. The pain of losing him still lingered, but it was tempered by the joy of remembering the love we shared. Of having him there with me. It was a bittersweet feeling.

"Bay," Shae said after a while, his tone more serious. "There's something I need to tell you."

Each beat of my heart reverberated through my body, creating a deafening thud in my ears. "What is it?"

"This place," he began, gesturing to the dreamlike world around us. "It's not just a figment of your imagination. It's a realm where souls linger when they have unfinished business."

"You mentioned something about that."

"You are my unfinished business, Bay. I've been waiting here for you. I cannot move on because you haven't found closure."

"You're saying that... wait. What exactly are you saying?"

"I need to know you're going to be okay before I can go. You're not okay. You haven't been okay since I left. So I'm here. Let me help you find closure. Because I can't leave you until you do."

"Oh." It was all I could manage. I tried to process his words and I couldn't decide if they made me more sad or angry. It was probably some combination of both.

"There's also one more thing," Shae said with a ravenous look in his eyes.

What was worse than being stuck here in limbo because the band aid won't stick to my heart like it was supposed to?

"What is it?" I asked, my voice quavering.

Shae's eyes darkened, and his voice grew husky. "I. Need. You."

All the anxiety left my body, replaced with a warming sensation. "Did you miss me?" I bit my lip.

Shae nodded vigorously. "I missed every single curve of your hips," he said, lifting my shirt and kissing my belly. His hands moved up my side and cupped my breasts. "I missed Bea and Arthur." The Golden Girl reference never failed to make me smile.

With a swift motion, he glided my shirt off my arms and casually discarded it. With no bra on, I could feel the cool air caressing my exposed breasts. I felt a sudden rush of arousal as his tongue traced a tantalizing path over my hardened nipples. With a gentle hand, Shae assisted me in standing, slowly unzipping my pants. He traced his hands down my body, his gaze fixated on every contour, savoring the anticipation like a child unwrapping a Christmas gift.

Shae always made me feel like the prettiest woman in the room. It was as if he couldn't wrap his head around the fact that someone like me would even acknowledge him. It was bonkers. Out of the two of us, I was the lucky one.

I pushed off his over shirt, feeling the smooth fabric slide against my fingertips, and slipped my hands under his t-shirt, relishing the warmth of his skin. His creamy skin stood out against my darker complexion. The sight of him, with his dark hair covering every inch of his body, sent a shiver down my spine. There was something about men who exuded the warmth of a werewolf that I found irresistible.

His beard tickled my fingertips as I gently traced my hand through it, feeling the wiry strands between my fingers. "I've missed you so much." As I unbuttoned his pants, they slipped down his backside, pooling around his ankles. With his boxer briefs now discarded, he stood completely naked before me.

"Me next," Shae's voice deepened, and he swiftly positioned himself between my legs, sensually removing my panties. "I want no barriers between us, nothing unsaid." His touch traced a tantalizing line from the inside of my thigh to the sole of my foot, igniting a wave of desire within me. "And definitely no clothes."

As Shae carefully placed me on the blanket, I could feel the warmth radiating from the magically sun-soaked fabric. His touch sent a surge of warmth coursing through me as his fingers explored the intimate heat between my thighs. "You're so wet. I want to taste you, Bay."

I nodded enthusiastically.

He spread my legs apart and found my folds. Using his tongue, he sensually licked and flicked my clit. Without warning, his teeth found their way to the sensitive skin of my inner thigh, causing me to gasp in shock.

"More, baby," I pleaded.

With a gentle touch, Shae slipped two fingers inside me, expertly caressing my G-spot, sending waves of pleasure through my body. He continued to stimulate my clit relentlessly, causing a growing pressure to build within me. I felt a tight coil building inside me until it finally released, resulting in an explosive and euphoric orgasm.

"I missed watching you come. Watching you wiggle with pleasure. I missed the sweet taste of you, baby."

Chapter Four

In a secluded inlet accessible only by foot, Shae proposed to me. It was nestled among jagged rocks, with the sound of water gently caressing the shore, and the faint scent of salt hanging in the air. His gaze lingered on me, his eyes filled with a love that spoke volumes. Shea knelt down on the jagged rocks, carefully holding a small box in his hand.

"Baylin Winters," he said, his voice trembling with nerves, "will you do me the honor of becoming my wife?"

I found his eyes. "Shae Travis, of course I'll marry you!"

As we stood in that spot, his fingers intertwined with mine, the overwhelming memory came rushing back.

"Do you remember this?" he asked, already knowing the answer.

Tears welled in my eyes. "How could I forget? It was the happiest moment of my life."

"And it still can be," he said, gently wiping away my tears with a brush of his finger. "These memories are etched into the very fabric of your being, inter-twining with this place. But they don't have to hold you back. Like a warm breeze that never fades, they can be carried with you, providing an endless source of strength and love."

"Let go of the guilt?"

Shae smiled. "Baylin, I want you to know that I am incredibly proud of you. You're stronger than you know."

In that fleeting moment, as the twilight bathed us in its radiant glow, we stood together, feeling the palpable force of our love.

The past and the present intertwined, creating a tapestry of love and loss, of pain and hope. A flicker of peace and a faint whisper of rebirth seemed to sing in the air.

The streets of Coral Cove stretched out before us, each step echoed with the memories of a life we shared. The town itself was a living, breathing scrap-book of our love story. I could feel Shae's presence beside me, grounding me, giving me the strength to take the next step.

We walked past the old movie theater where we had our third date. With over a hundred years of history, the theatre stands as a testament to its enduring legacy. The floors of the theatre recess into the ground, adding a unique architectural element to its design. The smell of popcorn and candy clung to the air. I remember the way Shae held my hand, squeezing it nervously during the scary parts, his thumb gently stroking mine. I teased him about it afterward, his boyish grin lighting up the night.

Shae held the door open for me, and we stepped inside the ghost theater.

"Do you remember the first movie we watched together?" I asked, glancing at Shae.

"Duh," he replied, a smile playing on his lips. "It was that truly terrible horror movie, the one with the ridiculous special effects."

I laughed. "You were so scared, you nearly jumped out of your seat."

Shae chuckled, "I wasn't scared, I was just...overly cautious."

We stepped into the larger of the two theater rooms. The bottom of the aisle boasted a grand stage, commanding attention. I released my grasp on Shae's hand, happily skipping down the vibrant red carpet and ascending the steps leading to the grand stage.

Shae followed behind me. He wrapped his hands around my waist and whispered in my ear. "I'm want to fuck you on this stage, Bay."

Heat pooled in my belly and moved between my legs. My clothes were gone in an instant, blurring boundaries between what was real and what was magic.

I reached for his pulsating cock and glided my

hand over the length of him. Taking control of the situation, Shae removed my hand abruptly and proceeded to secure both of my hands above my head, ensuring that I was unable to break free. In that moment of submission, I willingly surrendered myself to the experience and allowed it to consume the entirety of me.

Starting with a gentle kiss on my neck, he continued to trail his kisses down my body. He moved across my collarbone and finally reached my breasts. I ached for him. My entire being yearned to feel him deep inside me, to be wholly consumed by the intimate connection we shared.

Sex with Shae had always been mind-blowing. Before him, my experience was limited to the guy in my high school bio lab. I met Shae the summer after graduation. We'd been together for six years. Six years to memorize each other's bodies. Six years to learn every place that would drive the other wild. Six years with my best friend.

"Is this okay?" he asked in a husky voice.

With great enthusiasm, I nodded my head vigorously. "I need to feel you inside of me right now."

His lips met mine, and our tongues danced. The longing for him consumed me entirely, as every single inch of me craved the embrace and closeness of every single inch of him.

With a single motion, he pushed his thick, pulsating cock all the way inside.

A gasp escaped my lips, followed by a moan of pleasure.

With each thrust, he pushed deeper into me, harder than before—with more force. My eyes rolled to the back of my head. My body arched with every thrust. Inside of me, there was a growing bubble of warmth.

Leaning in towards me, he nibbled on my neck, still holding my arms above my head. He thrust into me again. The coiling inside of me grew tighter and tighter with each thrust until a tornado of pleasure ripped through me. The intensity of the moment overwhelmed me, causing me to cry out in ecstasy. Shae came inside of me, filling me with his liquid warmth, finding his own way to euphoria. He continued to pump inside of me three more times, and I rode the euphoric waves of our pleasure.

We stayed like that together for a long while. I didn't want the moment to end. But like all moments in time, they eventually do.

"I love you, Bay."

"I love you too."

But like all moments in time, they eventually do. I realized that this miraculous reunion came at a cost. An emptiness settled inside of me. Holding him like this would never be enough for me. I was on a journey to face my pain and free it. But at what cost?

Chapter Five

We left the theater and continued walking through the ghostly streets of downtown. Each step taking us through a parade of shared memories.

We reached the Spellbound Stories bookstore. I tried the door, and it opened. "Lea?" I asked to the void.

"No one else is here, my love," Shae reassured me.

I'd spent countless hours in this place, fingers brushing against the spines of books, debating what new adventures to take, what new authors to explore.

"Do you remember our favorite corner of this place?" Shae asked. As we got closer, his step gained a noticeable bounce to it.

I nodded, feeling a lump in my throat. "We used to sit there for hours, reading and sharing sexy passages from books we hadn't read yet. Until Lea or

Park would make us buy something or kick us out," I giggled.

He led me to that very corner. With a relaxing sigh, we settled ourselves onto the worn-out cushions, feeling the years of use beneath us. The memories of our time together were so vivid that I could almost hear the echoes of our laughter and the soft murmurs of our voices.

"Baylin," Shae said, his voice steady and deep. "This place, these memories... they're a part of who you are. If you won't take my word for it, find a way to forgive yourself."

"It's hard. I've been trapped in this infinity loop for so long," I said, swallowing the lump in my throat.

Shae took my hand and brought it to his lips. "I love you so much. You need to understand how debilitating holding that guilt inside is. You won't find happiness until you let it go."

We reached the edge of the town, where the twilight sky met the horizon. The world seemed to shimmer with a soft, iridescent glow, a symbol of the transformation that was taking place within me.

As I turned to face the town once more, a soft wind blew, carrying with it the scent of sea salt and lilacs. The air seemed to shimmer, and the world around me began to shift and change.

"Shae?" I spun around. "Shae? Where are you?" He wasn't there anymore.

Shae was gone.

Thick cement walls suddenly emerged from the

ground, seemingly out of nowhere, right in the heart of town. High edges casting long shadows in the endless twilight, and I found myself standing before a labyrinth. The entrance loomed before me, an archway of cold, dark cement. A warning to the journey I was about to undertake.

A familiar voice softly called my name, as if it were being carried on the wind and meant only for my ears. To my surprise, Shae's spirit materialized right next to me. "This labyrinth represents your path to acceptance and rebirth. You must navigate it alone, but I'll be here to guide you when I can."

I nodded in agreement, took a deep breath, and said, "I'm ready." Then I stepped into the labyrinth.

Chapter Six

As Shae's spirit faded, leaving me alone in the labyrinth, the air grew colder, and the light dimmed further. The surrounding vines thickened, their tendrils seeming to pulse with a life of their own, blocking my path back and urging me forward. Each step felt heavier, as if the weight of my past was pressing down on me, forcing me to confront what lay ahead.

The first memory materialized before me—It was dark, and foreboding. The scene unfolded with a clarity that was almost painful.

I was back in my childhood home. The familiar scent of cedar and old books filled the air. I saw my younger self, no more than ten years old. Standing in the dimly lit living room, I could see the soft glow reflecting off the brown carpets and baby blue curtains. My parents were there, their faces twisted in anger and disappointment.

"How could you let this happen, Baylin?" my father's voice boomed, echoing through the room. "You were supposed to watch over her!" Dad scrambled for a phone to call 911.

As I glanced to the corner, my heart sank at the sight of my younger sister, Lily. She was lying on the couch, her body fragile and complexion unnaturally clammy. Her breaths were shallow, her eyes closed. For weeks, she had been sick, and it had fallen on me to take care of her while our parents were at work. But I had been careless and distracted by my own interests. Like calling my girlfriends on the phone.

"She needed you." My mother's voice was softer but no less cutting. "And you failed her."

Guilt shredded through me, just as it had all those years ago. I had been so consumed with my own desires, wanting to escape the responsibilities thrust upon me, that I had neglected Lily. And it had nearly cost her life.

The memory became more twisted with each passing moment, causing the shadows surrounding me to ominously expand in size. The room morphed into a hospital ward, sterile and cold. I saw Lily again, older now, lying in a hospital bed, her condition having worsened over the years. The doctors spoke in hushed tones, words like "chronic" and "incurable" piercing through the fog.

"It's all your fault," the shadowy figure of my guilt whispered, taking form beside me. "If you had just been more responsible, more attentive, she wouldn't be suffering like this."

I clenched my fists, the weight of my guilt nearly overwhelming. I had spent so many years trying to make amends, trying to be better, but the shadow's words cut deep, reopening wounds I thought had long healed.

"No," I said, my voice trembling but resolute. "I was a child, and I made mistakes. And I've spent my life trying to make up for them, trying to be the person she needed."

The shadow loomed closer, its presence suffocating. "She still died."

"It wasn't my fault. I didn't make her sick. I was so young, I should have never had to watch her. She was sick, and that wasn't my fault."

The shadow hesitated, its form flickering like a dying flame. I took a deep breath, gathering all my strength. "You don't control me," I said firmly. "You're a part of my past, but you don't define my future."

With those words—the shadow that had loomed over me suddenly dissipated, its darkness receding and shrinking into the corners of my mind, granting me a newfound sense of clarity and peace. The oppressive weight lifting.

The labyrinth around me seemed to react to my resolve, the walls shifting and opening up a new path. I took a step forward, feeling lighter, freer, even if I knew the journey was far from over.

Unexpectedly, a chill ran through the air, and in that very moment, Shae kissed my neck. He nibbled my ear and tasted me. "You're doing wonderful, baby. I'd like one last taste of you."

A moan escaped me.

Shae slid his fingers down my body, slipped his hand inside of my pants and found my pussy. He put two fingers inside of me.

I gasped.

With deliberate slowness, he moved his fingers from my body. "Just one last little taste to remember you by," Shae said, taking his fingers into his mouth. "Mmmm baby, you're so sweet. Someone else is going to love the taste of you as much as I do."

"You think so?" I asked.

"I know so."

Chapter Seven

As I bravely forged ahead, the labyrinth's twisted pathways seemed to pull me deeper into a realm of terrifying nightmares that awaited me at every corner.

The next challenge appeared as I rounded a corner of the labyrinth. The air was crisp, carrying the scent of autumn leaves and the distant hint of rain. I watched a shadow of myself at the bakery, kneading dough and preparing for the day ahead. The memory of that day was seared into my mind, as if the pain of it had etched itself permanently into my soul.

Shae had popped into the bakery to tell me about his new project. He was a skilled architect and had taken on a renovation of a historical building in town. That morning, I was feeling down because the radio station rejected my pitch for a new show.

"Do you want me to stay home? I could play hooky and we could order take out, watch movies," Shae offered. A hint of mischief danced within his eyes.

The words I regret more than anything come tumbling out of shadow me's mouth. "No, no. I'll be okay, really. You do what you do best."

"If you insist," he said.

"I do."

"Don't work too hard, Bay," he teased, before kissing me on the lips. It was our last kiss. "I'll be back before you know it."

"I won't," I promised. "Be careful, okay?"

"I always am," he said, giving me one last lingering look before he disappeared out the back door.

The world shifted, as though the shadow world was moving on fast forward. It showed me the passage of time.

Dorothea was on the phone. She hung up and wiped a tear. "Baylin," she said, voice trembling. "There's been an accident. Shae... he's at the hospital."

I dropped the tray of muffins. They tumbled to the ground, scattering across the floor of the bakery kitchen. The world shifted and now we stood in the hospital. I don't remember the drive there. Like a frigid current flowing through my bloodstream, fear gripped me with its icy touch.

"Ms. Winters?" a doctor asked gently.

"Yes? Where's Shae? I need to see him." The words quickly spilled out of me in a rush as I anxiously asked, "Is he okay?"

"Ms. Winters," she said again. This time, she placed a hand on my arm.

I wanted to slap it away and scream just to tell me, but I didn't.

"I'm so sorry. Shae didn't make it."

Her words knocked the breath out of me.

"He sustained an injury to the head. Unfortunately, in surgery, his heart stopped beating and all attempts to revive him were unsuccessful. We did everything we could. I'm so sorry, but Shae is dead."

The gruesome details had come later, in bits and pieces. A massive wooden beam, improperly secured, had come loose and fallen, crushing Shae beneath it. The weight of it had been too much, the impact instantaneous. I couldn't bear to think of the pain he must have felt in those final moments, the shock and terror. Being alone.

And the guilt. Oh, the guilt. It consumed me, gnawing at my insides like a relentless beast. I could have told him to stay. He's still be alive if I would have made him play hooky.

If I delayed him a little longer, maybe he wouldn't have been there at that exact moment. If I insisted, he double-check the safety measures. If, if, if... The possibilities were endless, and each one was a dagger to my heart.

"Its all your fault," the shadow figure whispered in

my ear. "You could have saved him. He'd be alive if you weren't so selfish."

As I turned to face the shadow, tears streamed down my cheeks, overwhelmed with emotions.

"Stop lying to yourself," the shadow taunted.

"I am," I said with more gumption. "This whole time I thought it was my fault that Shae died. But it wasn't. It wasn't my fault that the beam fell. It wasn't his fault, either. Sometimes life is bigger than me. It wasn't my fault."

The shadow seemed to shrink in on itself, its form losing its glow and substance before vanishing entirely.

Finally, I reached the heart of the labyrinth. A clearing bathed in soft, golden light awaited me. In the center stood a mirror, its surface reflecting not just my physical form, but the entirety of my journey. I saw myself as I was—broken and healing; lost—but finding my way.

Shae's spirit appeared beside me. His presence brought a smile to my lips. I realized he was no longer the end all be all. It was an odd feeling to reconcile. But I knew it was right.

"You must look in the mirror and see yourself for who you truly are. Accept your past, your pain, and your strength. Every element contributes to defining the person who you are.

My heart was racing in my chest as I mustered up the courage to approach the mirror. I looked into its liquid depths. Memories came to life and swirled around me—both the joyous and the painful. I saw the love Shae, and I shared, the grief of his loss, and the journey I had to undertake to find healing.

My chest cracked open, and all my emotions came pouring out of me faster than I could process. Every moment of joy and every moment of sadness interlacing until I couldn't separate the emotions anymore. They were all tied together. I could never experience the bad without first experiencing all the good we shared.

The mirror shimmered and the labyrinth around me dissolved. The golden light enveloped me, filling me with warmth and peace. I whispered the words, "I accept it all."

As the light faded, I found myself back in Coral Cove, standing at the edge of the town.

Shae's spirit stood beside me one last time. He was radiant. "I love you so much, Baylin."

I nodded, feeling a sense of closure and rebirth move through me. "I love you too, Shae."

"Promise me you're going to live your life, Bay. Promise me you're going to find love again."

"I promise," I said, brushing a hand along his jaw.

"I will always be with you here," Shae placed his hand on my heart. "You are going to do amazing things with your long, long life, Baylin Winters."

"Can I get the lotto numbers?" I asked conspiratorially.

"One, one, two, three, five, eight—"

"That's the Fibonacci seque—"

Shae's mouth was on mine, cutting me off. It was a slow and dreamy kiss. This man owned a piece of my heart, and in some ways, I think he always would.

As our kiss ended and he disappeared from my arms. When I blinked again, I was back in the Arcane room.

Chapter Eight

When I awakened back in the small white room, a profound sense of peace had moved through me. I blinked, disoriented for a moment, before my memories of the labyrinth settled in my mind and reconciled with my life. It was like pieces of a puzzle finally coming together.

Ms. Vesper was standing nearby, her kind eyes watching me with a knowing smile. "Welcome back, Baylin," she said tenderly. "How do you feel?"

I took a deep breath, letting the air fill my lungs with a sense of calm I hadn't felt in a long time. "I feel... lighter," I admitted.

She nodded with understanding. "The journey you undertook could not have been an easy one. But I have a feeling it was a necessary one."

I sat upright, my body feeling somehow rejuvenated. "Thank you. I don't know that I'll ever be able to express my gratitude properly."

She waved a hand dismissively; her smile widening. "There's no need for thanks, my dear. You've done all the hard work. Now, it's time to take what you've learned and apply it to your life."

I felt a sudden surge of determination coursing through my veins. "I will."

I headed home to change and prepare myself for the next step. Despite experiencing previous rejection from the radio station, I was determined to approach them again today and not accept no for an answer. I knew exactly what I wanted, and I was ready to fight for it.

Once I arrived home, I wasted no time in freshening up and carefully selecting a professional yet comfortable outfit to wear. The feeling of anticipation filled my heart, knowing that this was the exact moment I had been waiting for. This was my chance to make a change, to turn the page and begin a fresh chapter in my life.

When I arrived at the radio station, I braced myself before walking in. I would not be turned down again.

The receptionist's polite smile did not conceal her surprise when she saw me entering the room.

"I'm here to see Richard Rhimes," I said, my

voice steady. "I don't have an appointment, but it's important."

The receptionist hesitated for a moment before picking up the phone. "One moment, please." After a brief whispered conversation, she looked up and nodded. "Mr. Rhimes will see you now." She buzzed me through the door.

The familiar hallway greeted me with a comforting scent of freshly polished wood as I walked its length. Every step was the sound of my resolve hardening. I knocked on Mr. Rhimes's office door.

"Come on in," he said, looking up from his desk, expression curious. "Baylin, it's good to see you. What brings you here today?"

"I have an idea for a radio show," I began, taking a seat across from him. "Picture a late-night talk show, where I connect with callers and use tarot cards to uncover secrets and offer guidance. Additionally, I would provide detailed horoscope readings, including insights into love, career, and health. It's something unique that I believe will draw in a lot of listeners."

Mr. Rhimes leaned forward in his chair. He laced his fingers together, eyebrows raised. "That's an interesting concept. Why do you think it will work?"

I smiled, letting my passion for the idea shine through. "People are fascinated by the mystical and the unknown. Tarot readings and horoscopes have always had a broad appeal. By combining theme with a live, interactive format, we can create something engaging and unique. Plus, my background and personal experience with tarot add a layer of authenticity that listeners will connect with. We can have guest speakers who can deep dive on a topic. I have a few people in mind already."

He studied for me a moment, then nodded. "I must admit, it's a compelling idea. And I can see the passion you have for it."

As I leaned forward, my heart raced with excitement. "I promise I won't let you down. I know I've been here before, but this time is different. I'm different."

Mr. Rhimes smiled, a genuine warmth in his eyes. "You really brought that sparkle today, Baylin. Let's hope you can bring it on air, too."

I nearly burst with excitement. "Oh, my gosh! You won't regret this. I promise."

"I hope not," he said. "I have an open slot at five pm on Friday nights. If it goes well, we can talk about expanding the show. Consider this a trial run."

A feeling of achievement and renewed hope surged through me as I left the radio station. For the first time since Shae's death, I felt truly good.

The sun beamed down from a cloudless sky as I made my way home, casting a warm glow on everything around me. I knew there would still be challenges ahead, but I was ready to face them. I felt equipped to embrace whatever the future held.

This was my rebirth, my new beginning. And I was ready to live my life fully, just as Shae had wanted.

KEEP READING for Baylin's Lemon Croissant Recipe!

SIGN up for Jax Wilder's newsletter and receive a collection of unpublished Coral Cove short stories. Meet familiar characters and dive deeper into the love and romance that Coral Cove is known for. Don't miss out on this exclusive content!

Explore Baylin's First Coral Cove appearance in Knead You Now and keep your eyes out for her next in On Air Affection in the Coral Cove series.

Knead You Now
A sweet mix of passion and pastry.

DOROTHEA

Early mornings, delicious pastries, and the comforting rhythm of kneading dough make up my world. But everything I've worked for is threatened I'm desperate and out of options. I turned to the town's most feared and successful lawyer, for help. Little did I know that accepting his assistance would come with an unexpected proposition – pretending to be his girlfriend.

LORENZO:

Coral Cove was supposed to be a fresh start, a place where I could build my own practice and escape the shadow of my overbearing father. But when he decides to visit, I need to show him I've settled down. Our arrangement is simple – I'll help her keep her bakery, and she'll help me convince my father that I'm living the life he envisions. But as we spend more time together, our fake relationship starts to feel all too real.

JOIN DOROTHEA and Lorenzo on a journey of love, trust, and the power of community. Will they be able to keep up their charade without falling for each other, or will the lines between reality and pretend blur beyond recognition?

Perfect for fans of heartfelt romances, small-town settings, and delicious baked goods. If you love stories where love blossoms in the most unexpected places, "Knead You Now" will warm your heart and satisfy your craving for a sweet romance.

Baylin's Lemon Croissant Recipe

For the Croissant Dough:

- 4 cups all-purpose flour
- 1/2 cup granulated sugar
- 2 teaspoons salt
- 1 tablespoon active dry yeast
- 1 1/2 cups warm milk
- 1/2 cup unsalted butter, melted
- 1 cup unsalted butter (for laminating), cold and cut into thin slices

FOR THE LEMON FILLING:

- 1/2 cup granulated sugar
- Zest of 3 lemons
- 1/4 cup fresh lemon juice
- 2 tablespoons cornstarch

- **For the Lemon Glaze:**
- 1 cup powdered sugar
- 2-3 tablespoons fresh lemon juice

INSTRUCTIONS:

PREPARE THE CROISSANT DOUGH:

1. In a large mixing bowl, combine the flour, sugar, salt, and yeast.
2. Gradually add the warm milk and melted butter, mixing until a dough forms.
3. Knead the dough on a lightly floured surface for about 5-7 minutes until smooth and elastic.
4. Place the dough in a greased bowl, cover with a damp cloth, and let it rise in a warm place for about 1-2 hours or until doubled in size.

PREPARE THE LEMON FILLING:

1. In a small saucepan, combine the granulated sugar, lemon zest, lemon juice, and cornstarch.
2. Cook over medium heat, stirring constantly, until the mixture thickens into a bright, tangy paste.

3. Remove from heat and let it cool to room temperature.

LAMINATE THE DOUGH:

1. Once the dough has risen, punch it down to release the air and roll it out into a large rectangle on a lightly floured surface.
2. Arrange the cold, thin slices of butter evenly over the dough.
3. Fold the dough over the butter like an envelope, ensuring the butter is completely enclosed.
4. Roll the dough out again into a large rectangle, then fold it into thirds. This is the first turn.
5. Wrap the dough in plastic wrap and refrigerate for 30 minutes.
6. Repeat the rolling, folding, and chilling process two more times, for a total of three turns.

SHAPE THE CROISSANTS:

1. After the final chilling, roll the dough out into a large rectangle (about 1/4 inch thick).
2. Cut the dough into triangles (base of each triangle should be about 4 inches wide).

3. Spread a small amount of the lemon filling on each triangle, being careful not to overdo it—just enough for a burst of lemony goodness without compromising the structure.
4. Starting from the base of the triangle, roll each piece up towards the tip, forming the classic croissant shape.
5. Place the rolled croissants on a baking sheet lined with parchment paper.

PROOF THE CROISSANTS:

1. Cover the croissants loosely with a clean kitchen towel and let them proof in a warm place for about 1-2 hours or until they are puffy and have doubled in size.

BAKE THE CROISSANTS:

1. Preheat your oven to 400°F (200°C).
2. Brush the tops of the croissants with an egg wash (1 egg beaten with 1 tablespoon of water).
3. Bake for 15-20 minutes or until the croissants are golden brown and crispy.

PREPARE THE LEMON GLAZE:

1. While the croissants are baking, mix the powdered sugar and lemon juice in a small bowl until smooth.
2. Adjust the consistency by adding more lemon juice or powdered sugar as needed.

GLAZE THE CROISSANTS:

1. Once the croissants are done baking, let them cool on a wire rack for a few minutes.
2. Drizzle the lemon glaze over the tops of the warm croissants, adding an extra touch of sweetness and tartness.

Enjoy these delightful lemon croissants with their perfect balance of buttery richness and bright lemony burst. They're best enjoyed fresh, but they also keep well for a day or two in an airtight container. Happy baking!

Also by Jax Wilder

CORAL COVE SERIES

Sleighed by Love

Harvesting Love

Dawning Desire

Knead You Now

TAROT FANTASIES SERIES

The Devil's Temptations

Strength of The Beast

Hanged Passions

Six of Cups

Death's Embrace

Additional Books by Rainbow Quartz Publishing

Additional Titles:

MIRANDA LEVI

From A Youth A Fountain Did Flow

The Sea Withdrew

A Tear In Time

Mo(ther) Na(ture)

In Orion's Hands

Jackson Anhalt

From The 911 Files

LORELAI HAMILTON

Find Your Bliss

Teenage Witch's Grimoire

Tarot Reflection Journal

Tarot Refection Journal Coloring The Tarot

The Eclectic Witch's Grimoire

Dream Journal

Teenage Tarot

Tarot Tales and Magic Spells

Arcane In Verse

ISLA WATTS: A FAIRY BAD DAY

Surprise! You're a Vampire

Gorgeous, Gorgeous, Gorgons

Mork The Handsome Orc

Adopted By Werewolves

Bite Me If You Can

That's The Spirit!

ROSE DAWSON'S BOOK JOURNALS: MY TIME WITH THE FAIRIES

Enchanted Escapades

Enchanted Escapades

Dewey Decimal Diaries

Siren's Songbook

Pride and Prejudice

Bibliophile's Bounty

Book of Books Journal

Pages & Passages Reading Journal

Bookworm's Companion Reading Journal & Tracker

About the Author

Jax Wilder is a passionate romance author hailing from a charming small town nestled in the picturesque Pacific Northwest. With a heart full of love and an unyielding belief in the power of happily ever afters, Jax weaves enchanting tales of love and connection that leave readers captivated.

Jax's novels are a reflection of her commitment to celebrating the magic of love, and her characters' journeys mirror the warmth and happiness she has found in her own life. Join her on the enchanting journey of love, passion, and enduring connection through her heartfelt romance novels.

www.ingramcontent.com/pod-product-compliance
Lightning Source LLC
Chambersburg PA
CBHW030511130626
46549CB00007B/2935